DR XARGLE'S
BOOK OF
EARTH RELATIONS

DR XARGLE'S
BOOK OF
EARTH RELATIONS

A Red Fox Book

Published by Random House Children's Books
20 Vauxhall Bridge Road, London SW1V 2SA

A division of Random House UK Ltd
London Melbourne Sydney Auckland
Johannesburg and agencies throughout the world

Text © Jeanne Willis 1993
Illustrations © Tony Ross 1993

1 3 5 7 9 10 8 6 4 2

First published in 1993 by Andersen Press

Red Fox edition 1995

Printed in Hong Kong

RANDOM HOUSE UK Limited Reg. No. 954009

ISBN 0 09 943251 X

DR XARGLE'S
BOOK OF
EARTH RELATIONS

Translated into Human by Jeanne Willis
Pictures by Tony Ross

Red Fox

Good morning, class. Today we are going to learn about Earth Family.

An Earth Family is a collection of Earthlings who belong to each other whether they like it or not.

They are many different ages from brand new to antique.

They have identical earflaps and hooter shapes.

A family begins with a mummy Earthling and daddy Earthling and one Earthlet.

The number of relatives in an Earth Family is always larger than the number of chairs at Christmas time.

A family row begins with two Earthlets called Bother
and Sulker.

Bother Earthlets are smelly, sticky and dangerous.
Never look in their pockets.

For supper they eat wiggly worms.

Sulker Earthlets are sly and sneaky and can be
recognised by their piercing shrieks.

To make them do this drop a webby eight legs down their frillies.

They squirt many gallons of water from their two eyes.

Here are Aunty and Uncle Earthling. When they come to visit, the Earthlets must frisk them on the doorstep for expensive gifts.

The Uncle Earthling is forced to crawl about on all fours like a neddy.

Everybody has to play a game called "Be quiet. We are talking". The winner is the last one to fall asleep.

Here are some phrases I would like you to learn:
"Gosh, is that the time?"
"We really must be going."

These are Grandpa and Grandma Earthling. They were born on Planet Earth at the same time as Tyrannosaurus Rex.

They are made from soft, crumpled material.

The Grandma Earthling grows fruit and flowers on her head.

At night, she puts pink hedgehogs in her fur. The
Grandpa Earthling puts his fangs in a glass.

Earthlets and ancient Earthlings behave in the same way. Here they all are at a bread-throwing competition. The winner is the one who hits the most ducks without falling in.

The most popular game is called "Where did I put my glasses?" This is something the whole family can enjoy.

That is the end of today's lesson. Put your disguises on quickly. Matron has kindly arranged for us to meet a real Earth family.

Have you all got your wedding invitations?

We will be landing at Buckingham Palace in five seconds.

Some bestselling Red Fox picture books

THE BIG ALFIE AND ANNIE ROSE STORYBOOK
by Shirley Hughes
OLD BEAR
by Jane Hissey
OI! GET OFF OUR TRAIN
by John Burningham
DON'T DO THAT!
by Tony Ross
NOT NOW, BERNARD
by David McKee
ALL JOIN IN
by Quentin Blake
THE WHALES' SONG
by Gary Blythe and Dyan Sheldon
JESUS' CHRISTMAS PARTY
by Nicholas Allan
THE PATCHWORK CAT
by Nicola Bayley and William Mayne
MATILDA
by Hilaire Belloc and Posy Simmonds
WILLY AND HUGH
by Anthony Browne
THE WINTER HEDGEHOG
by Ann and Reg Cartwright
A DARK, DARK TALE
by Ruth Brown
HARRY, THE DIRTY DOG
by Gene Zion and Margaret Bloy Graham
DR XARGLE'S BOOK OF EARTHLETS
by Jeanne Willis and Tony Ross
WHERE'S THE BABY?
by Pat Hutchins